P9-DNK-483

Riches to Rags

Based on the episode "The Baker King,"
by Laurie Israel and Rachel Ruderman

Adapted by Susan Amerikaner

Illustrated by Character Building Studio
and the Disney Storybook Art Team

DISNEY PRESS
Los Angeles • New York

Copyright © 2015 Disney Enterprises, Inc. All rights reserved. Published by Disney Press, an imprint of Disney Book Group. No part of this book may be reproduced or transmitted in any form or by any means, electronic or mechanical, including photocopying, recording, or by any information storage and retrieval system, without written permission from the publisher. For information address Disney Press, 1101 Flower Street, Glendale, California 91201.

First Paperback Edition, May 2015   10 9 8 7 6 5 4 3 2
ISBN 978-1-4847-0699-2

G658-7729-4-15166

Library of Congress Control Number: 2014954322
Manufactured in the USA
For more Disney Press fun, visit www.disneybooks.com

SUSTAINABLE
FORESTRY
INITIATIVE

ertified Sourcing

www.sfiprogram.org
SFI-01415

Sofia is happy.
It is almost time for the Villagers'
Ball.

Violet will go to the ball.
She helps Sofia get dressed.

The king has lots to do before
the ball.
He must open the new school.

He must fix the playground.
The garden needs work, too.
The king is very busy.

Sofia wants to help.
She helps the king choose
the new court jester.

The king has more to do.
He orders the cake for the ball.
"A baker does not work this hard,"
he says.

"I wish I were a baker."

The next day Sofia wakes up.
She is not in the castle.

Her family is in the village!

A man comes to buy bread.
"But I'm the king," says the king.
"Ha-ha!" says the man. "You are
the village baker!"

"Dad made a wish in front of the magic mirror," says Sofia.
"We must break the spell," says Amber.

But the king still wants to be a baker.
"I will not be so busy," he says.
"All I have to do is bake."

Sofia and the queen teach
everyone how to bake.

The king makes a big mess!
He tries again.

A mom stops to buy bread.

She pays too much!

Sofia finds the mom.
She returns some money.

The mom says everyone loves the
king for the new playground.
He needs to know this!
Sofia has a plan.

Sofia and the king go out.
They visit the playground.
They see the garden he grew.
What a happy village!

But the teacher at school is
not happy.
"The king did not come to open
the school," she says.

The king feels bad.
He must fix this.
"Time to break the spell," he says.
"How?" says Amber.

The king must go to the castle.
He must get to the magic mirror.
He must wish to be king again.

But first there is work to do.
The baker must make the cake
for the ball.
"We will bring it to you soon,"
says Sofia.

"This will be hard work," says the queen.

"A hard job is worth doing!" says the king.

The cake is ready!
They bring it to the castle.

Sofia and the king go to the
magic mirror.
The king wishes to be king again.
The spell is broken!

The people cheer.
The king is happy.
It is time for cake!

"This cake tastes bad," says the king.
"We must talk to the baker!"
Sofia and the king smile.